THE ROSES
IN MY
CARPETS

THE ROSES
IN MY
CARPETS

by Rukhsana Khan
illustrated by Ronald Himler

Fitzhenry & Whiteside

First published in Canada in 1988 by Stoddart Kids

First published in paperback in Canada by Fitzhenry & Whiteside in 2004

Published in Canada by Fitzhenry & Whiteside
195 Allstate Parkway
Markham, ON L3R 4T8

www.fitzhenry.ca   godwit@fitzhenry.ca

10 9 8 7 6 5 4 3

National Library of Canada Cataloguing in Publication Data

Khan, Rukhsana
Roses in my carpets
ISBN 0-7737-3092-3 (hardcover) 1-55005-069-9 (paperback)
PS8571.H37R67   1988   jC813'.54   C98-940479-5
PZ7.K42Ro   1988

Fitzhenry & Whiteside acknowledges with thanks the Canada Council for the Arts, and the Ontario
Arts Council for their support of our publishing program. We acknowledge the financial support of the
Government of Canada through the Canada Book Fund (CBF) for our publishing activities.

Printed and bound in Hong Kong, China by
Book Art Inc., Toronto.

To Kareem,
and all child refugees,
and for all the people who work with them
— R.K.

For Malcolm and Peggy
— R.H.

It's always the same. The jets scream overhead. They've seen me. I'm running too slowly, dragging my mother and sister behind. The ground is treacherous, pitted with bomb craters. My mother and sister weigh me down. A direct hit. Just as I'm about to die, or sometimes just after, I awake.

Blessed darkness. A moment passes before I realize I am in our mud house in the refugee camp. Safe. I hear the quiet breathing of my mother and sister nearby.

A cock crows, and then the eerie cry of the muezzin calls me to prayer. Dawn. I might as well rise and fetch the water before there is a lineup at the well.

My breath floats in clouds before me as I return with the heavy bucket. The plastic handle cuts into my hand. I must stop and rest several times.

At home I wash my face — a useless habit. Here, the walls are mud, the floor is mud, the courtyard is mud, too. It is impossible to stay clean.

I wake my mother before I go to the mosque for prayer. When I get back, breakfast is ready. My sister Maha still sleeps, so I eat my bit of bread and sip my tea in peace. Then I kiss Maha's sleeping face and go to school.

I hate school — a room full of restless boys — girls are in another class. We sit on rough mats that rub my ankles raw. I'd rather be weaving carpets.

When I come home for lunch, the hut is swept. I eat slowly, breaking the bread into pieces, making it last. Maha wolfs down her share, then eyes mine.

"No," says Mother sternly. But when her back is turned, I give Maha a few bites. I will pull my sash a little tighter.

Again, the muezzin calls me to prayer. Forgetting to be watchful, I step into the narrow road. A car brushes past, blasting a warning. In this place they drive as if demons pursue them, heedless of those in their path. I think of Maha. She, at least, is safe at home.

After Zuhr prayer comes my favorite time of day. I go to practice my skill as a carpet weaver. When I am weaving I can escape the jets, the nightmares — everything. As if with my fingers I create a world the war cannot touch. A paradise like the one where my father is.

My father was a farmer, at the mercy of weather or anyone who would steal his land and crops. But I will have a skill no one can take away. As long as I am strong and able, my family will never go hungry.

First I must practice. Someone far away makes my training possible. I am a sponsored child. A foster child. They even took my picture.

Soon, I will be a master craftsman and my sponsor's money will not be needed. I will hold my head high for the sake of my father who died ploughing our field in the war. He would never have taken aid from a sponsor.

Each color that I weave has a special meaning.

The threads that line the frame, on which all the other threads are knotted, are white. White for the shroud we wrapped my father's body in. Black is for the night that cloaks us from enemy eyes. Green is the color of life. Blue is the sky. One day it will be free of jets.

Everything in camp is a dirty brown, so I do not use brown anywhere in my carpets.

Red is my favorite. Red is the color of the blood of martyrs. But it is also the color of roses. I have never grown flowers. Every bit of land must yield food. So I make sure there are plenty of roses in my carpets.

I weave intricate patterns of roses, each connected to the other like the tribes of Afghanistan. A garden of beauty surrounded by a border, a wall. A wall around a little piece of paradise.

I am so intent on my weaving I do not hear the gasping breath of the boy who has entered the room. It is the silence that alerts me. I look up. Everyone is staring at me. Something is terribly wrong.

"It's your sister. She's been hit by a truck."

I leap to my feet and spill a thousand threads on the floor. A friend says to leave them, he'll pick them up. I nod and run out the door.

The runner tells me Maha is at the clinic. My mother is with her. They are operating, trying to save her legs.

When I arrive, my mother is frantic, trying to reach Maha. People are holding her back. There is screaming. It's coming from me.

My mother turns, her eyes wild. Like when my father died.

I must be strong. I must not cry. Gently I take her aside, telling her she is in the way. She nods. My words sink in. She puts her head on my shoulder and I see that I've grown. A strange time to notice such things. I tell my mother to go home and pray for Maha's safety.

When there is news, I'll come.

I cannot just sit and wait. I pace. Then I take my own advice and pray. I pray for Maha and for my mother. Then I pray for my sponsor who is paying for Maha's operation and doesn't know it. Afterward, I feel better.

Finally, the doctor emerges from the doorway looking haggard. Good news. Maha will be all right. Her legs are broken, but she will be able to walk again. Not soon, but one day. Relief washes over me like a cool rain. I run home to tell my mother. She looks old. She weeps for joy.

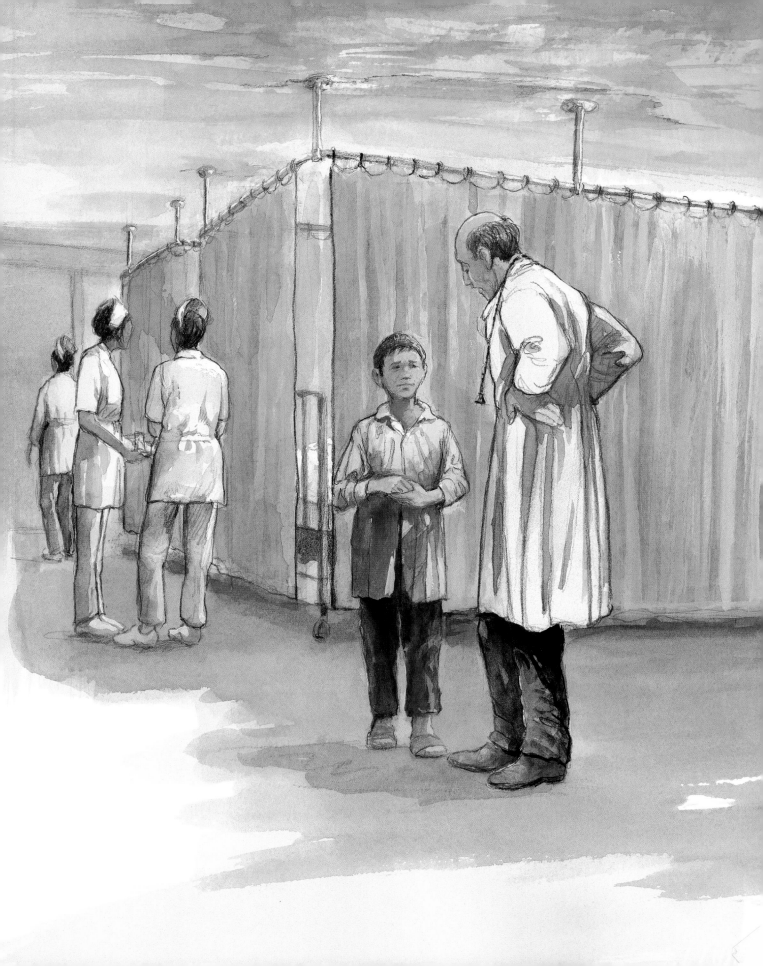

We have bread and water for supper. Mother rips the bread into three pieces before she remembers there are only two of us tonight. She gives me Maha's share. I give half of it back. In silence we eat. Every bite sticks in my throat. No amount of water helps.

Exhausted, I lie down on the straw mat that is my bed. It is too quiet without Maha. I miss her terribly. For a long time I cannot sleep.

When I finally do, I dream again of jets, tearing the fabric of the sky.

But this time my mother and sister do not drag at me. They run with me and do not hold me back.

While running, we find a space, the size of a carpet, where the bombs cannot touch us.

Within that space there are roses.